Written and designed by Annie Simpson
Illustrated by Clare Fennell

Copyright © 2011

make believe ideas ltd

The Wilderness, Berkhamsted, Herts, HP4 2AZ, UK.
565 Royal Parkway, Nashville, TN 37214, USA.

www.makebelieveideas.com

HicKorY DicKorY Dock

Annie Simpson • Clare Fennell

make
believe
ideas

Hickory **dickory** dock,

the mouse **ran** up the Clock.

The Clock struck **one**,

the mouse ran down!

Hickory **dickory** dock.

Max ran **down** the Clock,

across the mat,

under the chair,

and into the KitcHen,

where Mommy Mouse was baking.

"But there's nothing to do," said Max.

"I'm sure you'll think of something," said Mommy Mouse.

"And tie your shoes before you have an accident!"

But Max had a better idea...

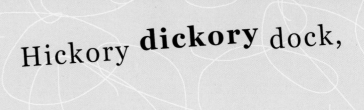

Hickory **dickory** dock,

the mouse **swuNg** from the CloCK.

The CloCK struck **two**,

he lost his shoe!

Hickory **dickory** dock.

"Is Kevin here yet?"

asked Max.

"No, not yet,"

said Mommy Mouse.

"Why don't you go and clean your room? And put your skates away – it's dangerous to leave them lying around!"

But Max had a better idea...

Hickory **dickory** dock,

Max **skated** down the **Clock**.

The **Clock** struck **three**,

he **baNged** his knee!

Hickory **dickory** dock.

"It's getting late. Do you think Kevin's lost?"

asked Max.

"No, I don't think he's lost,"

said Mommy Mouse.

"I'm sure he'll be here any minute. Why don't you wait for him in the yard?"

But Max had a better idea...

Hickory **dickory** dock,

the mouse **jumPed** off the ClocK.

The ClocK struck **four** – a **knock** at the door!

knock! knock!

Hickory **dickory** dock.

"Kevin's here!"

said Max.

"Okay! Sit nicely and do a puzzle together,"

said Mommy Mouse.

But Max had a better idea...

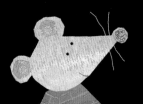

Hickory **dickory** dock,

the mice **dANced** round the **CloCK**.

The **CloCK** struck **five**, they **jigged** and **jived!**

Hickory **dickory** dock.

"When will dinner be ready?"

asked Max.

"Soon, Max. Why don't you help me find some cherries for the top of the cake?"

said Mommy Mouse.

Max found the cherries. But then he had a better idea...

Hickory **dickory** dock,

Max **juggled**

on the **Clock**.

The **Clo^cK** struck **six**

as he did

f_aN_cY

t_Ric**K**s!

Hickory

dickory

dock.

"Here they are, Mom!"

said Max.

"Thank you, Max,"

said Mommy Mouse.

"Now, put Kevin's bike in the garage, please – it looks like rain."

But Max had a better idea...

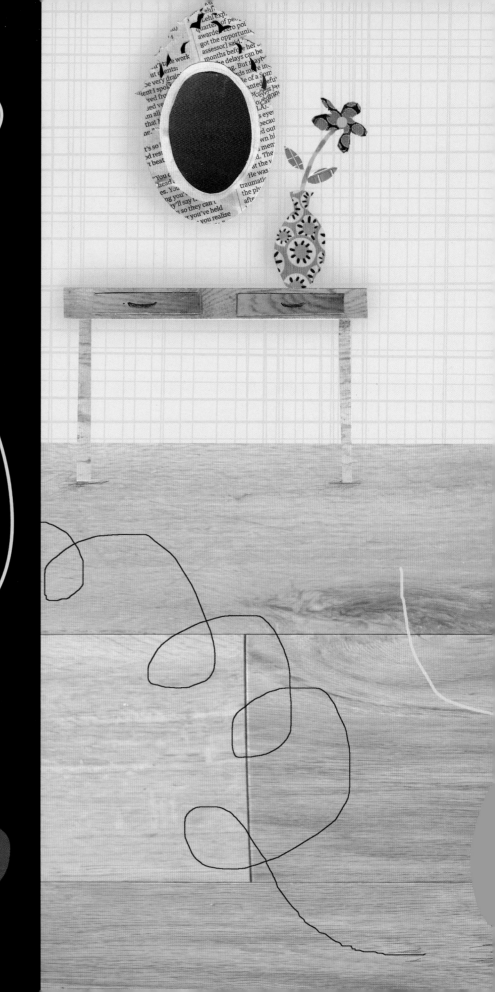

Hickory **dickory** dock,

they **cyc**L**e**D **down** the Clock.

The Clo**c**K struck **seven**,

"Be **careful**, Kevin!"

Hickory
dickory
dock.

"We're hungry!"

said Max.

"You can't eat anything now — you'll spoil your dinner,"

said Mommy Mouse.

But Max had a better idea...

Hickory **dickory** dock,

"There's **cheese** under the ClocK!"

The ClocK struck **eight**,

they just

couldn't wait.

Hickory

dickory

dock.

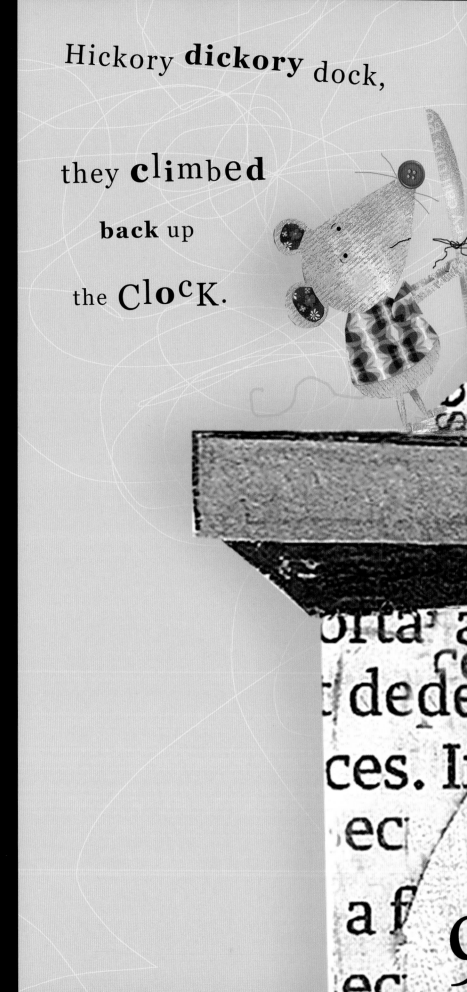

"Mom, we're bored!"

said Max.

"Well, if you're looking for something to do, why don't you set the table?"

said Mommy Mouse.

But Max had a better idea...

Hickory **dickory** dock,

they **climbed**

back up

the Clock.

The **Clo**C**K** struck **nine**   as they made a sign!

We want dinner!

Hickory

dickory

dock.

"Is it dinnertime yet?"

asked Max.

"Not long now!
Just time for you to do
some coloring,"

said Mommy Mouse.

But Max had a
better idea...

Hickory **dickory** dock,

the mice **jUMpeD** **over** the CloCK.

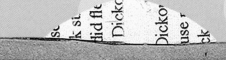

The CloCK struck **ten**, "Let's **do it again!**"

Hickory **dickory** dock.

"Dinnertime, boys!
I've made
cheese sandwiches,
cheese pizza,
cheese pancakes
and cheese cake,"

said Mommy Mouse.

"Now, come and
sit down."

And Max
thought that
was a great
idea...

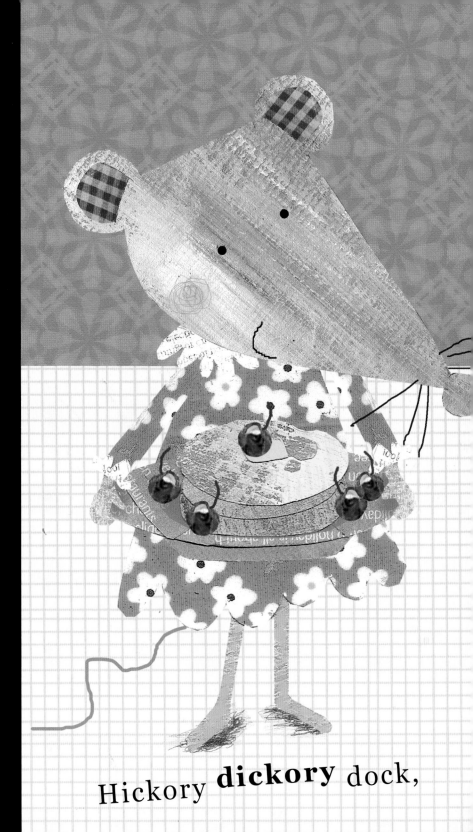

Hickory **dickory** dock,

they sat down by the clock.

The Cl**o**cK struck **eleven**,

"We're in **cheese heaven!**"

Hickory **dickory** dock.

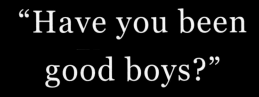

"Have you been good boys?"

asked Mommy Mouse.

"Yes, Mom,"

said Max.

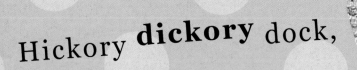

Hickory **dickory** dock,

the mice **r**a**N** up the Clock.

The ClocK

struck **twelve**...

Hickory **dickory** dock.